孩子的模仿力強，吸收力佳，在還沒形成地方口音之前，就讓他學習說英語，可避免晚一天學，多一天困難的煩惱！外國語言的學習，有助於智力的開發，及見聞的增長。前教育部次長阮大年說：「早學英語的好處很多。我小學四年級就開始學英語以致到了台灣唸中學，我一直名列前茅。」

「學習兒童美語讀本」1－3冊出版以來，各校老師都認為這套讀本活潑有趣的學習方式，可讓兒童快快樂樂地學會說英語。在各界的鼓勵下，我們配合教育部將英語列入國小選修課程的實施，企劃出齊「學習兒童美語讀本」全套六冊，使這套教材更趨完備。

對小朋友而言：本套書以日常生活常遇到的狀況為中心，讓小朋友從身邊的事物開始學英文。實用、生動而有創意的教材，小朋友更能自然親近趣味盎然的英語！

對教學者而言：本套書編序完整，教學者易於整理，各頁教材之下，均有教學提示，老師不必多花時間，就可獲得事半功倍的準備效果。此外，每單元均有唱歌、遊戲、美勞等活動，老師能在輕鬆愉快的方式下，順利教學！

對父母親而言：兒童心理學上，「親子教學法」對孩子學習能力的增強，有很大的幫助。本套書在每單元之後，均附有在家學習的方法，提供具體的方法和技巧，可以幫助家長與子女的共同學習！

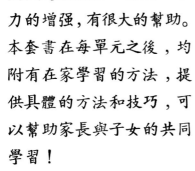

透過這套書，兒童學習英語的過程，必然是輕鬆愉快。而且，由於開始時所引發的興趣，未來的學習將充滿興奮與期待！

本 書 特 色

- 學習語言的基本順序，是由 Hearing（聽）、Speaking（説）、Reading（讀）、Writing（寫），本套教材即依此原則編輯。

- **內容背景本土化、國情化**，使兒童在熟悉的環境中學習英語，避免像其他原文兒童英語書，與現實生活有出入的弊端。

- 題材趣味化、生活化，學了立即能在日常生活中使用。

- 將英語歌曲、遊戲，具有創意的美勞，與學習英語巧妙地組合在一起，以提高兒童的學習興趣，達到**寓教於樂**的目的。

- 每單元的教材均有教學指導和提示，**容易教學**。而且每單元之末均列有目標說明，指導者易於掌握重點。

- 提供在家學習的方法，家長們可親自教導自己的子女學習英語，除加強親子關係外，也達到自然的學習成效。

- 每單元終了，附有考查學習成果的習作，有助於指導者了解學生的吸收力。

- 書末附有總複習，以加深學習印象。另外，在下一冊書的前面也有各種方式的複習，以達到溫故知新的目的。

- 本套書以六歲兒童到國二學生為對象，是全國唯一與國中英語課程相銜接的美語教材。學完六冊的小朋友，上了國中，既輕鬆又愉快。

Contents

Review 1 > Where are they?

Look and read.

My name is Mary. My room is at the top of our house. I am sitting by the window.

My mother is in the kitchen cooking dinner. My father is behind the car. He is washing the car in the middle of the yard.

My sister Helen is sitting on the sofa. She is sitting in front of the TV. A teddy-bear is under the TV. There is a tree at the side of my house. My dog is lying at the bottom of the tree. He likes to be near the kitchen.

Note : Review the prepositions like "on", "in", "by", "near", "under", "in front of", "in the middle of", "at the side of", "at the top of" and "at the bottom of".

Review 2 Present Progressive Tense

Look and say.

1. eat
2. eat an apple
3. cook
4. sleep
5. read
6. drink
7. swim
8. shout
9. fly
10. run
11. clap
12. wash

1. A: Is she eating?
   B: No, she isn't.
      She isn't eating.

   A: What is she doing?
   B: She is washing.

   A: What is she washing?
   B: She is washing her face.

2. A: Is the monkey eating an apple?
   B: No, it isn't.
      It isn't eating an apple.

   A: What is it doing?
   B: It is eating.

   A: What is it eating?
   B: It is eating a banana.

Note : This chart provides practice in the present progressive tense using phrases like "is eating" & "is washing" in contrast to the simple present tense.

Review 3 > Simple Present Tense

Look and say.

> What does John like ?
> He likes sports.
> Does he play soccer ?
> No, he doesn't. He plays basketball.

> Does Mary play volleyball after school ?
> No, she doesn't.
> Why not? Doesn't she like it ?
> Yes, she likes it. But she does her homework after school.

> Does your mother make breakfast ?
> Yes, she does.
> Does she make your bed ?
> No, she doesn't. I make my bed.

> Does your sister like math ?
> No, she doesn't. But she likes music.
> Can she sing ?
> Yes. She can sing.

> Who's that ?
> That's Mr. Brown. He teaches at my school.
> What does he teach ?
> He teaches English.

(Note) : You may wish to review "What does ~ " and "Does s(he) like ~ ". Let students practice reading the paragraph to each other. Circulate around the classroom. Listen for correct pronunciation and intonation.

Review 4 > Breakfast, Lunch & Dinner

A: What do you have for breakfast ?
B: I like jam and bread.

A: Do you eat rice for breakfast ?
B: Yes, I do. I eat rice.

A: Do you drink coffee ?
B: No, I don't. I don't drink coffee.

A: What do you like to drink ?
B: I like to drink milk.

How about you ?

Note : This chart offers practice in the question pattern: "What do you have ~".

Review 5 ⟩ Daily Life

Sing a song.

A. This is the way
I wash my hands,
wash my hands,
wash my hands.
This is the way
I wash my hands.
Early in the morning.

B. That is the way
he washes his hands,
washes his hands,
washes his hands.
That is the way
he washes his hands.
Early in the morning.

 This is the way I get up, ...

 This is the way I brush my teeth, ...

 This is the way I wash my face, ...

 This is the way I eat my breakfast, ...

 This is the way I go to school, ...

 This is the way I do my homework, ...

 This is the way I go to bed, ...

(Note) : Review everyday activities through this popular tune. The teacher can divide students into two teams: A & B. Let them take turns practicing this song and performing.

1 MY SCHOOL

Mary: How many grades are there in your school?
John: There are six grades.

1 WHAT GRADE ARE YOU IN?

John is eleven years old. He walks to school every day. Now it is seven o'clock in the morning. Wayne is his new friend. He is walking to school. They meet in the street.

John : Hello, Wayne.

Wayne : Hi, John. How are you ?

John : Fine, thank you. And you ?

Wayne : Fine, thanks. Are you going to school ?

John : Yes, I am. Where are you going ?

Wayne : I'm going to school, too.

John : Where do you go to school ?

Wayne : I go to Chung Shan Elementary School.

John : What grade are you in ?

Wayne : I'm in the fourth grade. How about you ?

John : I'm in the fifth grade.

Wayne : What time is your first class ?

John : It starts at eight o'clock.

Wayne : Okay, see you!

John : See you!

1-1 LET'S PRACTICE

Look and say.

A: How many days are there in a week?
B: There are seven days in a week.

apples (table)   cats (desk)   birds (tree)   chairs (window)

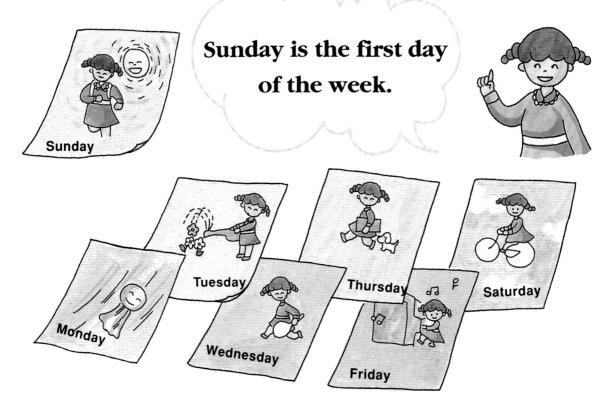

Sunday is the first day of the week.

Sunday

Monday

Tuesday

Wednesday

Thursday

Friday

Saturday

(Note): Review "how many" and "there are" until the students can change the sentences.

PLAY A GAME

A road game.

Let's start.

1. Go to the fourth square.

2. Go to the fifth square.

3. This bird is green. Color it. Then go to the eighth square.

4. The bear's ears are black. Color them. Then go to the sixth square.

5. The lion wants a tail. Draw it. Then go to the ninth square.

6. Go back to the third square.

7. The rabbit needs two eyes. Draw them. Then go back to the second square.

8. Go back to the seventh square.

9. This is the end.

EXERCISE

Read and write.

I am going to school.

_____?

I'm in the fourth grade.

What grade are you in?

Draw yourself here.

What time is your first class?

How many students are there in your class?

■ 在家學習的方法：家長可先利用書上的圖片教孩子一到六年級的說法，再和孩子做 "What grade are you in?" 的問答練習，等熟練之後，再問孩子其他人，如鄰居、哥哥、姐姐們唸幾年級。

■ 本單元目標：學習如何使用序數，尤其特別的『第一』、『第二』、『第三』、『第五』等，老師可多利用問句練習，讓小朋友回答自己的年級。

HAPPY BIRTHDAY TO YOU

Nancy :   Happy birthday to you, John!

John :   Thank you, Nancy.
          Mother told me to invite my friends to my
          birthday party.
          Please come to my house this afternoon.
          Mark, Tom and Susan will come to the party, too.

Nancy :   Thank you very much, John. I will be on time.

John :   See you later!

2 WHEN IS YOUR BIRTHDAY?

When is your birthday ?
his
her

My birthday is
on December fifteenth.

His birthday is
on June eleventh.

Her birthday is
on March twenty-second.

When is New Year's Day ?

It is on January first.

When is Christmas ?

It is on December twenty-fifth.

LET'S PRACTICE

Look and read.

The Calendar

October

Sun.	Mon.	Tue.	Wed.	Thu.	Fri.	Sat.
first **1**	second **2**	third **3**	fourth **4**	fifth **5**	sixth **6**	seventh **7**
eighth **8**	ninth **9**	tenth **10**	eleventh **11**	twelfth **12**	thirteenth **13**	fourteenth **14**
fifteenth **15**	sixteenth **16**	seventeenth **17**	eighteenth **18**	nineteenth **19**	twentieth **20**	twenty-first **21**
twenty-second **22**	twenty-third **23**	twenty-fourth **24**	twenty-fifth **25**	twenty-sixth **26**	twenty-seventh **27**	twenty-eighth **28**
twenty-ninth **29**	thirtieth **30**	thirty-first **31**				

(Note) : Teach the students how to say their birthday using dates.

2-2 PLAY A GAME

Answer and write.

A : When is your birthday?

B : My birthday is _____(date)_____

A : When were you born?

B : I was born on _____(date)_____ in _____(year)_____

MONTH	Jan.	Feb.	Mar.	Apr.	May	Jun.
NAME						
MONTH	Jul.	Aug.	Sept.	Oct.	Nov.	Dec.
NAME						

(Note) : Let the students take turns asking each other "When is your birthday?" and take notes.

EXERCISE

Look and write.

The Birthdays of My Family Members

Do you know these dates ?

A: What date is it today ?
B: _____

A: What day is it today ?
B: _____

■**本單元目標**：讓孩子能記得家人的生日，並能用英文表達。注意『月份』、『日期』
　的說法。

■**在家學習的方法**：媽媽可以拿家中的日曆做練習，隨時問他們"What day is
　today?" 或是"When is your birthday?"等複習。直到他們熟練。

3 HIM AND HER

He's my brother. I like him and he likes me.

That's right. I'm his brother. I like him and he likes me.

She's my sister. I like her and she likes me.

That's right. I'm her sister. I like her and she likes me.

(Note): Tell students the difference between "his", "her", "your" & "my". Give them some examples. When you feel the students have had enough practice with the above, let them make sentences.

 **3 THEM AND US**

They are my friends.
I like them and
they like me.

That's right.
We are his friends.
We like him and
he likes us.

They are my friends.
I like them and
they like me.

That's right.
We are her friends.
We like her and
she likes us.

LET'S PRACTICE

Look and say.

A : Who is this man ?

B : He is Mary's father. I like <u>him</u> very much.
Do you know Mary ?

A : Yes, I do. I know <u>her</u>. She knows <u>me</u> very well. We are good friends.

PLAY A GAME

Learn a rhyme.

1. **Look at the boy in the tree.**
   Can you see him ?
   Yes, I can see him.
   Look at the woman near the tree.
   Can you see her ?
   Yes, I can see her.

2. **Look at the clouds. They're very high.**
   Can you see them ?
   Yes, I can see them.
   Look at the bird in the sky.
   Can you see it ?
   Yes, I can see it.

3. **Look at the driver of the car.**
   He can't see me.
   He can't see you.
   He can't see us.
   But we can see him.

(Note) : If you feel students have had enough practice with this, ask them questions about the picture.

■本單元目標：練習they、we、he、she和them、us、him、her之分別。

■在家學習的方法：媽媽可用各種東西或家中人物來練習they them，we us等組合關係的差異。

3-3 **EXERCISE**

Write and circle.

① I know Mary's sister. But my mother does not know _____ .

② I like my dog. He likes _____ , too.

③ We like Mark. He likes _____ , too.

④ Does your father take_____ to the zoo ?
Yes, he sometimes takes me to the zoo.

⑤ Does Mark have an umbrella with _____ ? No, he does not.

⑥ A: How many hot dogs do you have ?
B: I have four.
A: Are (they, their, them) all for (you, your) ?
A: No. (They, Their, Them) are for John and (I, my, me). They are (we, our, us) lunch. (We, Our, Us) like (they, their, them) very much.

4 OUR, YOUR AND THEIR

Our dog is big. Your dog is small.
Our dog is young. Your dog is old.
Our dog is pretty. Your dog is ugly.
We like our dog.
We don't like your dog.

Your dog is small. Their dog is big.
Your dog is old. Their dog is young.
But I like your dog.
I don't like their dog.

IT'S YOURS

Mother : What are you doing, Mary ? It's already eight.

Mary : I'm looking for my umbrella.

Mother : Here, take this umbrella.

Mary : That is not mine. It's yours.

Mother : Yes. But you can use it today.

Mary : Thank you. Bye, Mom.

Mother : Bye, Mary.

I, MY, ME AND MINE

1.
I	am
You	are
He	is
She	is

a student.

We
You
They

are students.

2. These are

my
your
his
her
our
their

apples.

3. The teacher likes

me.
you.
him.
her.
us.
them.

3. The apples are

mine.
yours.
his.
hers.
ours.
theirs.

LET'S PRACTICE

Look and say.

(1)　A：Whose bird is this ?
　　　B：It's Mary's. The bird is hers.

Circle and say.

(2)

1. A：Is this your book ?
　 B：Yes, it is (mine, yours).

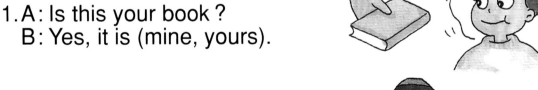

2. A：This pen is Susan's. Are those
　　　pens (his, hers), too ?
　 B：No, they are not. They are (her
　　　mother, her mother's).

3. A：How many friends do you have ?
　 B：I have two friends. (They, Their,
　　　Them) names are Mark and
　　　Nancy.

4-2　PLAY A GAME

The white cat is Susan's.

The black one is also hers.

Mark and Nancy have two birds.

The blue and yellow ones are theirs.

We also have a bird.

Ours is red and black.

What is it?

(Answer: a ladybird)

EXERCISE

Look and write.

(1)

Mary :   Good _____ , Miss Wang.

Miss Wang :   Hi, Mary. You have a beautiful umbrella.

Mary :   Oh, it isn't _____ .

Miss Wang :   Whose umbrella is it ?

Mary :   It's my _____ .
        I am using it today.

(2)

I	my			
you	your			
he		him	his	
she	her			
it	its		x	
Mary		Mary		

we		us	
you	your		
they			theirs

■本單元目標：練習所有主詞、代名詞、所有格、受詞等各種詞性的用法。讓學生瞭解彼此間的差異，然後練習造句。

■在家學習的方法：媽媽可事先準備一些道具，如鉛筆、水果等，再一邊指著鉛筆，一邊告訴孩子"This is your pencil.""This pencil is yours."給予他們所有格的觀念。再利用"You like me.""I like you."的句型，告訴他們me、us、them等的用法。

5 IT'S RAINING TODAY

Mary :   It's raining today.
Jack :   Do you like this weather?
Mary :   No, I don't like this weather.
Jack :   What are you doing?
Mary :   I'm reading a book.
Jack :   What book are you reading?
Mary :   I'm reading a story book.
Jack :   Where is your sister, Helen?
Mary :   She's in her room.
Jack :   What is she doing?
Mary :   She is studying history.
Jack :   Does she like history?
Mary :   Yes, she likes history very much.
Jack :   Well, it is getting dark. What time is it now?
Mary :   It's about six now.
Jack :   I'm going home now. Good-bye.
Mary :   Good-bye.

5 FOUR SEASONS

Spring is warm.
We play baseball in spring.
Spring brings flowers and
green leaves.

Summer is hot.
Summer brings sunshine.
We swim in summer.

Autumn is cool.
We play tennis in autumn.
Autumn brings the cool
wind and brown leaves.

Winter is cold.
We ski in winter.
Winter brings the falling
snow.

twenty-nine

LET'S PRACTICE

Look and say.

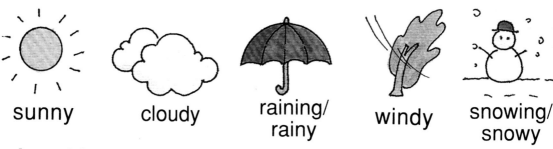

sunny	cloudy	raining/ rainy	windy	snowing/ snowy

A : How's the weather today ?
B : It is windy.
A : How was the weather yesterday ?
B : It was rainy.
A : How will the weather be tomorrow ?
B : It will be cloudy.

(Note) : Tell the students how to use the tenses and ask questions about the pictures.

 **SING A SONG**

You Are My Sunshine

You are   my   sun - shine, —— my on - ly sun-shine, ——

You make me   hap - py —— when skies are   gray.

You'll nev-er   know, dear,   how much I love   you.

Please don't   take   my sun - shine a - way.

Look and write.

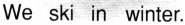

We ski in winter.

_____

_____

_____

Weather Report

It is rainy today.
I go to school.

_____

_____

_____

_____

_____

■**本單元目標**：學習各種天氣的表達方法。

■**在家學習的方法**：利用書上的圖表，教孩子 "It is ～" 的句型。平常上學前，也可用英文和孩子做「今天／昨天／明天天氣如何？」的問答。

6 ♠ I CAN RIDE A BICYCLE

Mary : Susan can walk.
I can ride a bicycle.
Jack can ride a motorcycle.
Mark can drive a car.

Mary : Are you busy today?
John : No, I'm not. I'm free today.
Mary : Fine, I'm going to the zoo now.
Can you ride a horse?
John : Yes, I can.
Mary : I'm going to the zoo with Jack, Mark and Susan.
John : Can I go with you?
Mary : Yes, you can. Please come with us.
John : Thank you. Are we going by bus?
Mary : Well, I can ride a bicycle. Jack can ride a motorcycle.
Mark can drive a car. You can ride a horse, and
Susan can walk. So we can all go together!

6 HOW DO YOU GO TO SCHOOL?

taxi   bus   bicycle

car   train

I go to school by bus.	I go to school by bicycle.	I go to school by car.

I go to school by train.	I go to school by taxi.	I go to school on foot.

■本單元目標：學習搭乘各式交通工具的說法。

■在家學習的方法：能流利說出如何搭乘各樣交通工具後，媽媽如能陪孩子一起用紙摺一些模型，一起配合練習，則更能加深他們的記憶。

 **6-1 LET'S PRACTICE**

Look and say.

A: Can you swim?
B: Yes, I can.
A: Can you cook, too?
B: No, I can't. But my mother
   can cook very well.

dance
play the piano

speak English
play baseball

ride a bicycle
ride a horse

ride a motorcycle
fly an airplane

drive a car
ride a horse

play basketball
play the violin

(Note): First teach the students how to ask and answer the questions on this page using
these pictures. Then recite all the verbs and make sentences.

6-2 PLAY A GAME

Make a boat.

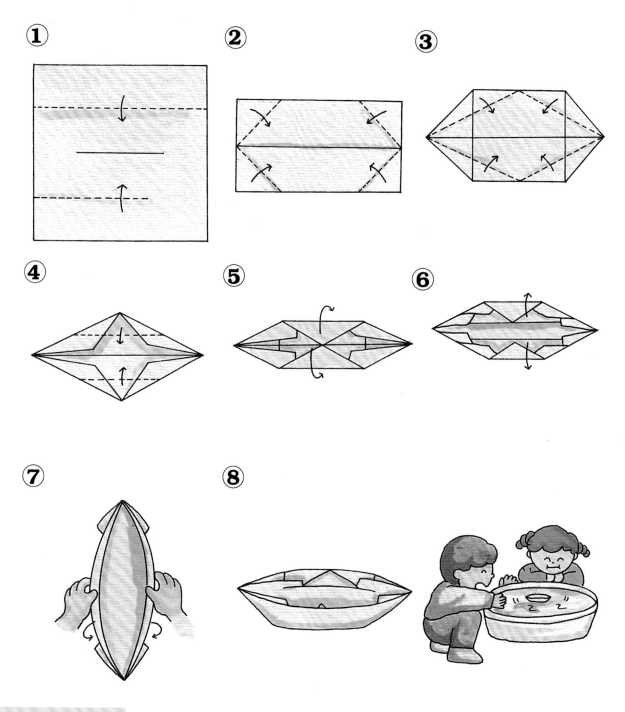

① ② ③

④ ⑤ ⑥

⑦ ⑧

EXERCISE

Write and say.

My name is _____ .
I am_____ years old.
I live in _____ .
I get up at _____ o'clock.
I go to school by _____ .
And I can _____ .
    What can you do ?

(Note) : Let all of the students introduce themselves one by one.

7 I AM OLDER THAN YOU

Mark : How old are you, Nancy?

Nancy : I am ten years old.

Mark : How old are you, Jack?

Jack : I'm twelve years old.

Mark : Who is older, you or Nancy?

Jack : I am older than Nancy.

Mary : Nancy is tall. She is taller than I.
　　　She is the tallest girl in our class.

John : Mark is very tall. He is taller than I.
　　　He is the tallest boy in our class.
　　　He is as tall as Nancy.

LET'S PRACTICE

Look and say.

> I am taller than you.
> You are shorter than I.

taller / shorter

bigger / smaller

older / younger

faster / slower

noisier / quieter

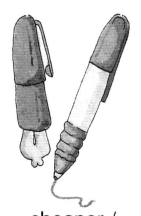

cheaper /
more expensive

(Note) : Teach students how to make sentences with taller / shorter, bigger / smaller, older / younger and so on.

A： Jack is older than Susan.
B： Susan is older than Nancy.
A： Jack is the oldest of the three.

old

older

oldest

good

better

best

long

longer

longest

big

bigger

biggest

beautiful

more
beautiful

most
beautiful

(Note) : Think of examples and make comparisons based on the pictures.

7-2 PLAY A GAME

Make a guess.

In my family, Father is stronger than my brother John.

My sister, Mary, is not stronger than I. I am as strong as my sister, Mary. John is stronger than Mary and I, but he is not stronger than Father and Mother. Father is stronger than Mary and I, but Mother is stronger than Father. Who is the strongest?

■本單元目標:練習比較級、最高級用法及差異。
■在家學習的方法:媽媽可以把全家人拿來做例子,試著讓小孩比較出誰最高、誰最胖、最小等等或將圖片蓋住讓小朋友自行說一遍再糾正其錯誤。

EXERCISE

Look and say.

1. Who is taller, John or Mary ?
John is _____ _____ _____.

2.

The elephant is _____ _____ the giraffe.
The giraffe is _____ _____ the dog.
The elephant is the _____ of the three.

3.

A is bigger _____ B.
C is _____ than B.
C is _____ _____ box.

4.

The bicycle is _____ _____ the motorcycle.
The motorcycle is _____ _____ the car.
The car is _____ _____ _____ of the three.

8 I WAS IN TAIPEI LAST YEAR

I was in Taipei last year. My parents and sister were there, too. But my brother John wasn't with us. He was in Tainan at that time.

Taipei was very crowded. There were a lot of people and cars. There were new buildings all over the city. It was a busy city.

8 I CALLED YOU LAST NIGHT

Tom :   I called you last night, but there was no answer.
Susan : Sorry. We were out last night.

Tom :   Oh?
Susan : We were at Mary's house. They invited us to dinner. Mary and I listened to some records. We stayed there until half past ten.

8 LAST NIGHT...

I **was** at home.

We **were** out.

She clean**ed** her room.

He play**ed** the violin.

I watch**ed** TV.

They listen**ed** to records.

Mother cook**ed** dinner.

Mary and John wash**ed** dishes.

Susan visit**ed** us.

Tom shout**ed** at me.

8-1 LET'S PRACTICE

Look and say.

A: What did you do on Sunday ?
B: I played baseball with my friends.

yesterday/
paint a picture

last Saturday/
play tennis

last night/
cook dinner

yesterday morning/
walk to school

A: Did you play tennis yesterday ?
B: No, I didn't. I didn't play tennis yesterday.

watch TV   play baseball   talk to John

visit Mark   listen to records   stay at home

(Note) : First teach the students how to ask and answer the questions on this page. Then practice on how to use the past tense. Let everyone answer the questions.

SING A SONG

OLD MACDONALD HAD A FARM

Old Mac-Don-ald   had   a   farm   E - I   E - I -

O!   And   on   his   farm   he   had   some   ducks

E - I   E - I   O! With   a   quack   quack   here   and   a

quack   quack   there   here   a quack, there a quack

Eve-ry   where   a   quack   quack   Old   Mac-Don-ald

had   a   farm   E - I   E - I   O!

8-3 EXERCISE

(1) Fill in the blanks (was or were).

Yesterday _____ Saturday.
It _____ fine and warm.
Tom _____ in the park with
his dog. It _____ a wonderful
spring day.
The flowers _____ beautiful.
The birds _____ in the trees.

(2) Make sentences.

① Mary / call / Susan (**yesterday**)

　　Mary called Susan yesterday.

② We / invite them / dinner (**last night**)

_____

③ Mark / wash dishes (**last night**)

_____

④ Mary / is / in Taipei (**last year**)

_____

⑤ She / clean the living room (**last Sunday**)

_____

⑥ They / listen to / records (**last night**)

_____

■本單元目標：練習過去式was, were用法及過去式動詞加ed的用法。
■在家學習的方法：媽媽可試著幫助小孩說出昨天或前天在學校所做之事，皆用過去式表達。

A HOLIDAY

Yesterday was Sunday. It was sunny and warm.

Mark got up early. He ate breakfast at seven o'clock. He went to the zoo with Jack and Peter. They went to the zoo by bicycle. There were many children at the zoo. Mark saw some lions and tigers. He liked them very much. Jack saw some big elephants, polar bears and horses. Peter also saw some birds and monkeys. Then they saw a tall giraffe. They were very excited. They talked to the giraffe. A parrot looked at them and said, "Hello!" They answered, "How are you?" They went around the zoo by bicycle. Then they went home at five o'clock. They all had a very happy holiday.

WHAT DID THEY DO?

1. I get up early.
I got up early yesterday.

2. John goes to school.
He went to school yesterday.

3. Helen eats her breakfast.
She ate her breakfast this morning.

4. Mark studies English.
He studied English last summer.

5. They have a farm.
They had a farm last year.

6. I come home.
I came home two hours ago.

7. Nancy sings a song.
She sang a song an hour ago.

8. They see an elephant.
They saw an elephant the day before yesterday.

LET'S PRACTICE

Read and practice.

A : Did Mark sleep well last night ?
B : Yes, he did. He was very tired.
A : Why ? What did he do yesterday ?
B : He rode his bicycle.

Mary
work hard

Tom
wash the windows

John
clean his room

Peter
study English

Susan
write letters

SING A SONG

Twinkle Twinkle Little Star

① Twinkle, twinkle, little star,

② How I wonder

③ what you are!

④ Up a —

⑤ — bove the

⑥ world so high,

⑦ Like a diamond in the sky.

EXERCISE

Look and write.

A: Did you go to a concert yesterday ?
B: No, I didn't.
A: Where did you go ?
B: I went to the movies.

A: Did you go to school by car the day before yesterday ?
B: No, _____ _____ .
A: How _____ _____ _____ to school ?
B: _____ .

A: Did you come home at 5:00 yesterday ?
B: _____ , _____ _____ .
A: When _____ ?
B: _____ .

A: Did you sing a song last night ?
B: No, _____ _____ .
A: What _____ _____ do ?
B: _____ .

A: Did you eat your breakfast yesterday ?
B: _____ , _____ did.
A: What _____ _____ _____ ?
B: _____ .

A: Did you see a tiger in the zoo ?
B: No, _____ _____ .
A: What _____ _____ _____ ?
B: _____ .

■本單元目標:過去式的不規則動詞變化,如went, ate等。
■在家學習的方法:先讓孩子們比較出過去式和現在式的不同。再利用反覆的代換練
　習,讓孩子們記住這些不規則的動詞變化。

10 I WAS RUNNING

Nancy: Were you out this morning?

Tom: Yes, I was. I was running along the river with my dog. Were you at home?

Nancy: No, I wasn't. I was looking for a present for my little brother.

Tom: Is that the present?

Nancy: Yes. It's "Mother Goose." It has a lot of beautiful poems and pictures.

10 HOW DID THEY DO IT ?

① How did John break his leg ?
He broke it while he was playing baseball.

② How did Susan cut her finger ?
She cut it while she was preparing dinner.

③ How did Tom lose his wallet ?
He lost it while he was playing baseball.

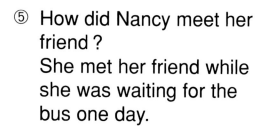

④ How did Helen's father cut himself ?
He cut himself while he was shaving.

⑤ How did Nancy meet her friend ?
She met her friend while she was waiting for the bus one day.

LET'S PRACTICE

Look and say.

A: Were you studying English yesterday evening?
B: No, I wasn't.
A: What were you doing?
B: I was watching television.

study English

watch television

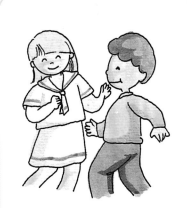

dance with my friends

play basketball

prepare dinner

write a letter

10-2 PLAY A GAME

Body quiz.

It has two arms.
It has a back.
It has two legs.
It has two feet.

It has a back.
It has arms.
It has a seat.
It has four legs.

It runs.
It has two hands.
It has a face.
It tells time.

It flies.
It has a tail.
It has wings.
It has a face.

■**本單元目標**：過去進行式的句型。
　　　　　 ⎰I was + Ving
　　　　　 ⎱They were + Ving
■**在家學習的方法**：先復習以前學過的現在進行式，再讓孩子將 be 動詞換成 was 或 were，即爲過去進行式。

EXERCISE

10-3

Look and write.

1 _____

2 Tom lost his wallet while he was washing his hands. _____

3 _____

4 _____

5 _____

6 _____

Write a sentence about yourself here. Then draw a picture of yourself.

11 WHAT ARE YOU LOOKING FORWARD TO?

Mary is looking forward to her birthday. Her friends are going to have a party for her. They will prepare a big birthday cake for Mary.

Tom and Mark are looking forward to this Sunday. They will go picnicking on Sunday. They will bring a lot of food and take a lot of pictures. They will go if the weather is fine.

John is looking forward to next weekend. They'll have a good party. He will meet some new people. Some will play games. Others will eat. Everyone will have a good time.

11-1 LET'S PRACTICE

Look and say.

John : Are you going to play baseball tonight?
Mark : No, I'm not. I played baseball yesterday.
John : What are you going to do?
Mark : I'm going to play tennis.

① Is Tom going to school tomorrow?
to swim

② Is Susan going to play the piano tonight?
see a movie

③ Are Paul and John going to play football tomorrow night?
to dance

④ Are Peter and Jack going to ride a bicycle next week?
to drive a car

⑤ Is Mary going to swim tomorrow afternoon?
to ski

⑥ Are Mark and Nancy going to eat ice-cream tonight?
to eat hamburgers

11-2 SING A SONG

The Sun Is Shining

11-3 EXERCISE

Read and write.

1. What is Mary going to do next weekend ?
2. What is Susan looking forward to tomorrow ?
3. Who is going to play baseball tomorrow afternoon ?
4. Who is going to buy a radio ?
5. Who is going to clean the room next Sunday ?
6. Who is going to watch television tonight ?
7. What are you going to do tonight ?

Mary _____ .

Susan _____ .

Peter _____ .

John _____ .

Nancy _____ .

Tom _____ .

■本單元目標：學習未來式「be going to～」的句型。
■在家學習的方法：先教孩子如何說「將要做～」的句型，熟練之後，再加上表示未來時間的說法，如next weekend, tomorrow morning等。

 # 12 JOHN'S TIMETABLE FOR TOMORROW

This is John's timetable for tomorrow.

6:30 Get up	9:40 Natural Science	3:00 Classroom Activities
6:40 Brush his teeth and wash his face	10:30 Social Science	4:00 Go home
7:00 Have breakfast	11:20 Math	4:30 Homework
7:30 Go to school	12:00 Lunch	6:45 Dinner
8:00 Arrive at school	12:30 Break	8:00 Watch TV
8:50 First period: Chinese	1:30 Art	9:30 Go to bed
	2:20 Physical Education	

Tomorrow John will get up at half past six. He will brush his teeth and wash his face at six forty. At seven he will eat breakfast. He will leave the house at seven thirty, and arrive at school at eight o'clock.

At eight fifty, he will go to his first class: Chinese. At nine forty John will have his Natural Science class. Social Science will begin at half past ten, and Math will start at eleven twenty.

At noon, John will eat lunch. He will finish at half past twelve, then take a break. Next he will have Art class at one thirty, Physical Education at two twenty, and Classroom Activities at three. At four o'clock, John will go home.

He will get home at four thirty and do his homework. Dinner will be ready at a quarter to seven. Afterwards, at eight, John will watch TV. He will go to bed at nine thirty.

I WANT TO BE …

Look and answer.

1. Who wants to be a scientist ?
2. Who wants to be a businessman ?
3. Who wants to be a doctor ?
4. Who wants to be an artist ?
5. Who wants to be a police officer ?
6. Who wants to be a teacher ?
7. Who wants to be a musician ?
8. Who wants to be a pilot ?
9. Who wants to be a lawyer ?
10. Who wants to be a singer ?
11. What do you want to be when you grow up ?

LET'S PRACTICE

Look and say.

A: Will you be home this evening?
B: Yes, I will.
   I will watch TV at home.

A: Will Mary be home this evening?
B: No, she won't.
   She will study hard at school.

1. Nancy

go swimming

2. Tom, Peter and Susan

play frisbee

3. Mary and John

go shopping

4. you

visit a friend in the hospital

5. your father

read newspapers

6. Helen

clean her room

(Note): This chart provides practice in forming questions in the simple future tense, using the verb "will".

PLAY A GAME

Find your way.

①
John, come to this table.
This is a clock.
What time is it now?

(x) → No, you are not right.
Sing a song.

(o) ↩

② (o)
Yes, you are right.
Here is your banana.
Go to Mary.
Who is taller, you or Mary?

(x) → No, you are not right.
Hand your banana to Mary.

(o) ↩

③ (o)
Yes, you are right.
Shake hands with Mary.
Walk to the blackboard.
Don't walk slowly. Run.
Where are you now?

(x) → No, you are not right.
Mary, draw a short line
on John's face.

(o) ↩

④ (o)
Yes, you are right.
Here is your apple.
Eat it.
How many girls are there
in this room?

(x) → No, you are not right.
Clean the table and the
blackboard.

(o) ↩

⑤ (o)
Yes, you are right.
Go back to your seat.
Sit down.

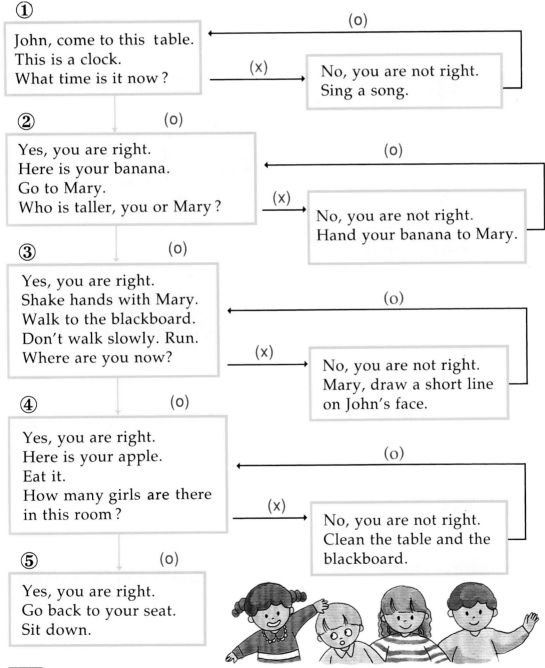

(Note) : Ask the students questions. If they get them right, then let them go on.

12-3 EXERCISE

Read and write.

Example:

A : Where will you be next weekend?
B : I will be in the park.
A : What will you do there?
B : I will take a walk.

A : Where＿＿＿ ＿＿＿ ＿＿＿tonight ?
B : They ＿＿＿ ＿＿＿ at home.
A : What ＿＿＿ ＿＿＿ ＿＿＿ there ?
B : They ＿＿＿ study English.

A : Where＿＿＿ ＿＿＿ ＿＿＿tomorrow?
B : ＿＿＿ ＿＿＿ ＿＿＿ ＿＿＿ home.
A : What＿＿＿ ＿＿＿ ＿＿＿there?
B : ＿＿＿ ＿＿＿ wash the kitchen floor.

A : ＿＿＿ ＿＿＿ ＿＿＿ ＿＿＿this evening ?
B : ＿＿＿ ＿＿＿ ＿＿＿ in the kitchen.
A : ＿＿＿＿＿＿＿＿＿＿＿＿＿ ?
B : ＿＿＿ ＿＿＿ bake cookies.

■**本單元目標**：未來式中will的使用。

　在家學習的方法：媽媽可教小朋友用自己的功課表，說出明天一天的活動。平時媽媽也可多問孩子類似「星期天要做什麼？」的問句，練習未來式will的句型。

Review 1 A Game

1. Look at page 33.
   What's Jack riding?

2. Look at page 1.
   What's under the T.V.?

3. Look at page 20.
   What can you see in the sky?

4. Look at page 11.
   Whose birthday is it?

5. Look at page 1.
   Where is Mary's mother?

6. Look at page 28.
   What is Helen studying now?

7. Look at page 12.
   Which month is Mary's birthday in?

8. Look at page 38.
   How many children can you see?

9. Look at page 49.
   Where is Mark going?

10. Look at page 51.
    What did Mark study last summer

11. Look at page 63.
    What's John going to buy?

12. Look at page 65.
    What does Susan want to be?

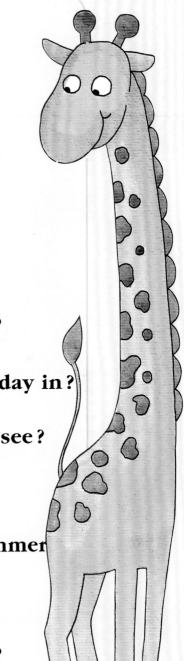

Review 2 〉 Oral Practice

Ask & Answer:

1. What grade are you in?
2. Where do you go to school?
3. How many days are there in a week?
4. When is your birthday?
5. Do you like your friends?
6. How many friends do you have?
7. What's the weather like today?
8. How was the weather yesterday?
9. How do you go to school?
10. Can you ride a bicycle?
11. Who is the tallest in your family?
12. Is your father older than your mother?
13. What did you do on Sunday?
14. Did you study English yesterday?
15. Were you playing basketball yesterday evening?
16. What are you going to do tomorrow?
17. Are you going to swim tonight?
18. Will your mother be at home next Sunday?
19. Will you study hard at school?
20. What do you want to be when you grow up?

Picture Dictionary

1. teddy-bear	2. carrot	3. clap	4. play volleyball
5. elementary school	6. calendar	7. study history	8. season
9. spring	10. summer	11. autumn	12. winter
13. sunshine	14. play tennis	15. ski	16. snow
17. sunny	18. cloudy	19. rainy	20. windy

21. snowy	22. motorcycle	23. horse	24. taxi
25. cook	26. dance	27. strong	28. beautiful
29. giraffe	30. my parents	31. crowd	32. city
33. wash	34. listen to records	35. dishes	36. children
37. polar bear	38. parrot	39. holiday	40. movie

41. present	42. look forward to	43. wallet	44. shaving
45. tail	46. wings	47. camp	48. mountains
49. hike	50. magazine	51. fix the car	52. timetable
53. Natural Science	54. Social Science	55. Math	56. Physical Education
57. Art	58. frisbee	59. hospital	60. kitchen

第 四 冊 學 習 內 容 一 覽 表

單元	內　　容	練　　　習	活　　動	習　　作
複習第三冊	(1) 他們在哪裏？ (2) 現在進行式？ (3) 簡單式 (4) 早餐、午餐和晚餐 (5) 日常生活	Look and read. Look and say. Look and say. Look and say. Sing a song.		
1	我的學校	Look and say：看圖練習 How many～? 與 first, second 等序數的問答。	遊戲：A road game	Read and write.
2	生日快樂	Look and read：看月曆學習日期的說法。	遊戲：When is your birthday?	Look and write.
3	他和她	Look and say：看插圖練習受格 him, her, me 等的用法。	遊戲：Learn a rhyme	Write and circle.
4	我們的，你們的和他們的	Look and say：從例圖中練習代名詞所有格 mine, yours, hers 的用法。	遊戲：Make a guess	Look and write.
5	今天是下雨天	Look and say：看圖練習 How's the weather today? 的問與答。	歌曲：You are my sunshine	Look and write.
6	你如何去學校？	Look and say：看插圖練習 can 的句型代換。	勞作：Make a boat	Write and say.
7	我比你大	Look and say：從給予的圖片中練習比較級和最高級的句型。	遊戲：Make a guess	Look and write
8	我去年在台北	Look and say：看圖練習過去式的句型問答。（規則動詞變化）	歌曲：Old MacDonald had a farm	① Fill in the blanks. ② Make sentences.
9	放假日	Read and practice：練習過去式的不規則動詞變化，看圖代換問答。	歌曲：Twinkle twinkle little star	Look and write.
10	我正在跑步	Look and say：看例圖練習過去進行式的句型問答。	遊戲：Body quiz	Look and write.
11	你正期待著什麼？	Look and say：看例圖練習未來式 be going to 的問與答。	歌曲：The sun is shining	Read and write.
12	約翰明天的功課表	Look and say：看圖練習未來式 will 的問與答。	遊戲：Find your way	Read and write.
複習	(1) 遊戲 (2) 口頭練習 (3) 生字總復習	A crossword puzzle Ask and answer Picture dictionary		

國立教育資料管審核通過！

學習兒童美語讀本④
LEARNING
English Readers for Children

書＋MP3 一片售價：280 元

編　　　著／陳怡平

發　行　所／學習出版有限公司　　☎ (02) 2704-5525

郵 撥 帳 號／05127272 學習出版社帳戶

登　記　證／局版台業 2179 號

印　刷　所／裕強彩色印刷有限公司

台 北 門 市／台北市許昌街 17 號 6F　　☎ (02) 2331-4060

台灣總經銷／紅螞蟻圖書有限公司　　☎ (02) 2795-3656

本公司網址／www.learnbook.com.tw

電 子 郵 件／learnbook@learnbook.com.tw

2023 年 8 月 1 日新修訂

ISBN 978-986-231-068-7